Attention,

Super Hero Squad fans!

Look for these items when you read this book.

Can you spot them all?

FIREWORKS

ROBOT

CLOUDS

MARVEL
SUPER HERO
SQUAD

Little, Brown and Company

Hachette Book Group
237 Park Avenue, New York, NY 10017
Visit our website at www.lb-kids.com

LB kids is an imprint of Little, Brown and Company. The LB kids name and logo
are trademarks of Hachette Book Group, Inc.

The publisher is not responsible for websites (or their content)
that are not owned by the publisher.

First edition: April 2011

10 9 8 7 6 5

ISBN: 978-0-316-08482-6

CW

Printed in the United States of America

CAPTAIN AMERICA
TO THE RESCUE!

by Lucy Rosen
illustrated by Dario Brizuela
coloring by Franco Riesco

LITTLE, BROWN & COMPANY
LB kids

All of Super Hero City
was buzzing with energy.
It was the day of the summer picnic.
That was the city's biggest festival.

There was food and music.
Best of all, Captain America
was hosting a
fireworks show later!

"Listen up, Super Heroes,"
said Iron Man.
"We have a lot of work to do
before the fireworks show starts."

"Thor, hammer away
at those tables.
Hulk, you're in charge
of building the stage.
Captain America and I
will go over his speech."

A Sentinel flew overhead!
Dr. Doom had sent
one of his evil robots
to spy on the Super Heroes.

The Super Hero Squad
was hard at work.
No one noticed the robot.

Dr. Doom snarled
as he watched the heroes
on the screen in his hideout.

"Perfect! No one is protecting
the fireworks," Dr. Doom said.
"Let's see how they like it
when I break up their little picnic!"

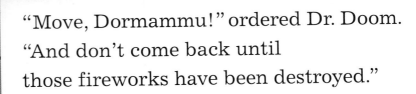

"Move, Dormammu!" ordered Dr. Doom.
"And don't come back until
those fireworks have been destroyed."

"Yes, sir," said Dormammu.
He knew exactly what to do.

Dormammu crept into
Super Hero City
and went over to
the fireworks storage shed.

Dormammu hid quietly
while the people enjoyed the picnic.
When the sun went down,
he knew it was almost time
for the fireworks show to begin.

"It's slime time!" said Dormammu.
He poured slimy green goo
all over the fireworks.

"Let's see what kinds of sparks fly now that the fireworks are all wet!" Dormammu chuckled.

Just then, Captain America and Iron Man
came in to set up the fireworks
and caught Dormammu!
Captain America acted fast.

He threw his shield.
It stopped the villain in his tracks.
"So nice of you to stop by,"
Captain America said.
"Too bad you can't stay."

"Colossus, take care of this guy,"
said Iron Man.
With one big throw,
Colossus pitched Dormammu
back to Villainville!

"What are we going to do about the fireworks?" asked Iron Man. "Everyone is waiting for the show to start!"

"I have an idea,"
said Captain America.
"I'm going to need
everyone's help."

Captain America told
the Squad his plan.
"Let's do it," said Iron Man.
"Time to Hero Up!"

Captain America gave Iron Man
a handful of fireworks.
Iron Man flew them
up into the night sky.

Then Thor used his hammer
to create a small rainstorm
right above the fireworks.
The rain washed away
all the slimy green goo.

"Your turn, Human Torch,"
said Captain America.

Human Torch heated up the air
around the fireworks
and dried them out.
Then he shot a fireball
to spark the fireworks!

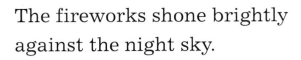

The fireworks shone brightly against the night sky.

All of Super Hero City
clapped for Captain America
and the Super Hero Squad.
They had saved the day!

Dr. Doom could see the fireworks
from the window of his lair.
"I'll get you someday,
Super Hero Squad!" he yelled.